Lexi Kinney

Buckaroo Chuck

Written by Lexi Kinney
Illustrated by Marinella Aguirre
ISBN 978-1-948543-51-4

Printed in the United States of America

To my sweet Anthony, the real Buckaroo Chuck!

Call me Buckaroo Chuck.
I'm a cowboy for reals,
Big hat on my head,
Spinning spurs on my heels.

Belt buckles galore
That spell out my name.
Can't wait to win more
In a rodeo game!

**Hobby horse,
Rockin' horse,
I practice all day.**

Sittin' high.
Holdin' tight.
I hear a loud "neigh!"

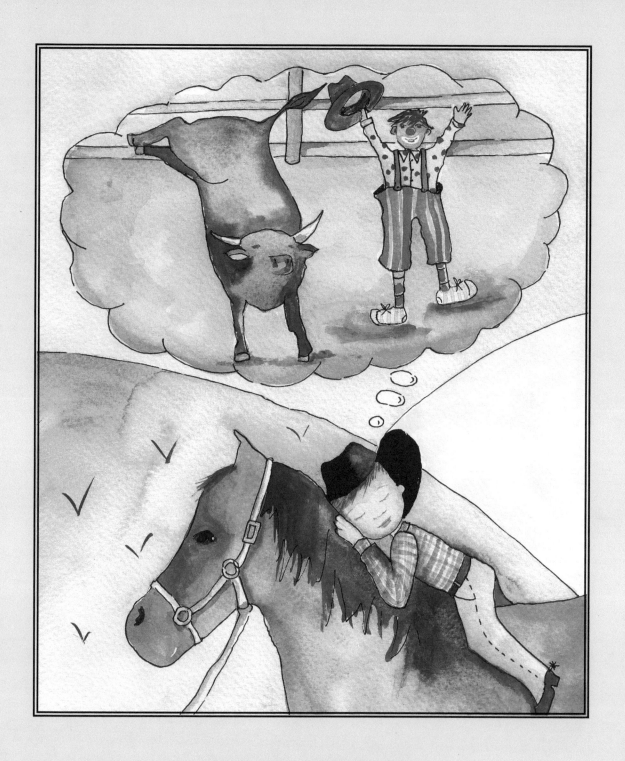

I dream of that day
When the show comes to town
With a big bucking bull
And a rodeo clown.

I'll give it my all;
Try as hard as I can.
'Cause someday I'll be
A big rodeo man.

My dad's got my back
As he walks by my side.
Into the arena
For my very first ride.

With my helmet and vest
I jump on a sheep,
Running 'round that big ring
As it kicks with a leap.

With my eyes open wide,
As that sheep runs around.
I'm gripping on tight
As we bounce up and down!

I hoot and I holler
When that mutton I bust.
I'm sittin' real pretty
'Til I land in the dust.

I'll give it my all;
Try as hard as I can.
'Cause someday I'll be
A big rodeo man.

With my helmet and vest,
I jump on a calf.
Running 'round the arena,
While I try not to laugh.

On the back of that calf,
One hand in the air,
I ride as it bucks
Like I haven't a care.

Only six seconds more
To show all my fans.
I'll finish real big
And they'll all clap their hands.

I'll give it my all;
Try as hard as I can.
'Cause someday I'll be
A big rodeo man.

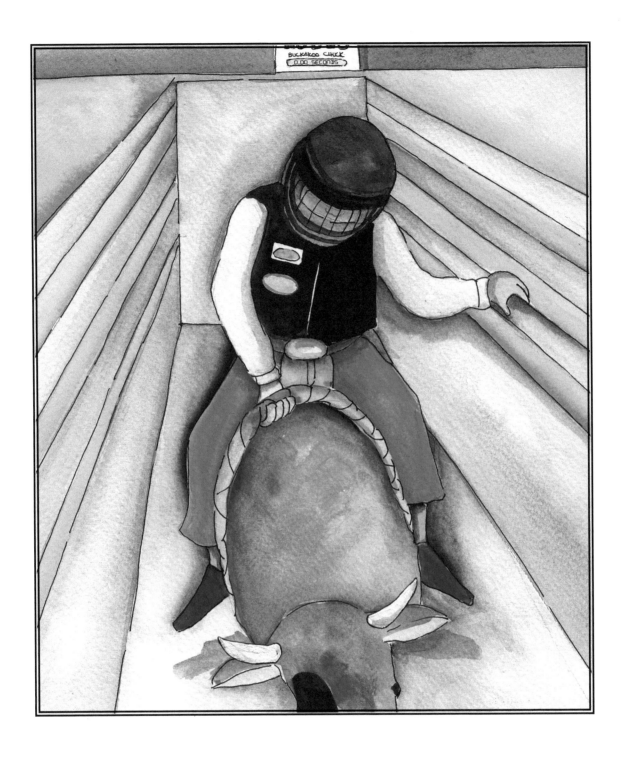

With my helmet and vest,
I jump on a steer.
I hang on real tight
As it kicks up its rear.

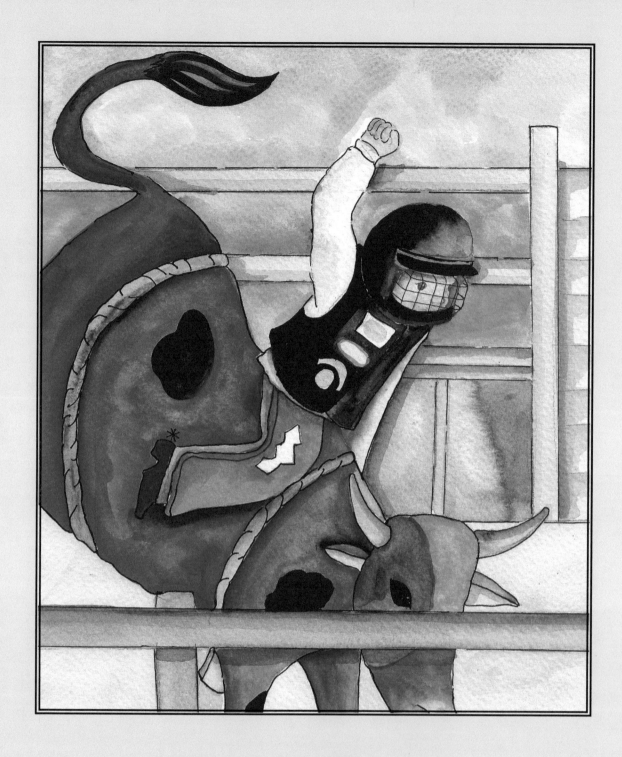

As it stomps and it bucks,
It's me and that steer.
I'm learning to ride
Without any fear.

I'll hang on if I can
For eight seconds or more.
I'll show all my fans
What I live my life for.

I'll give it my all;
Try as hard as I can.
'Cause someday I'll be
A big rodeo man.

Today is the day!
The show is in town
With the big bucking bull
And the rodeo clown.

23

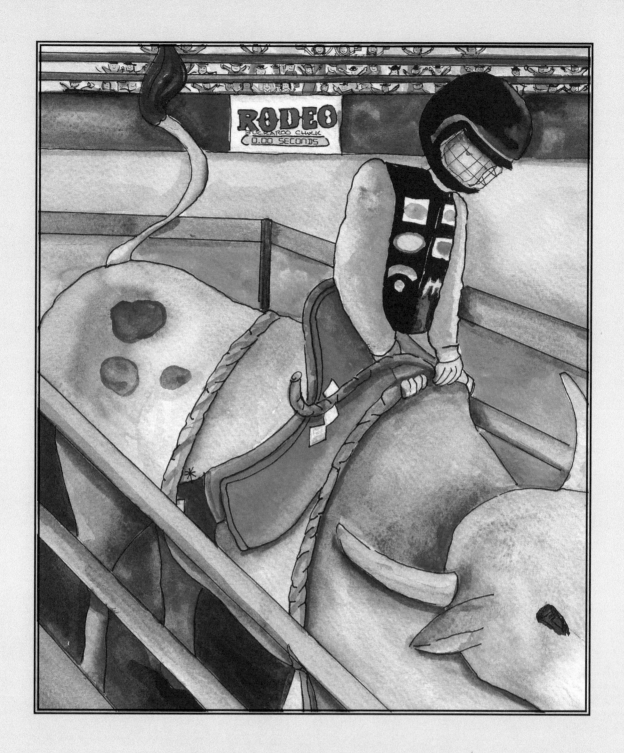

With my helmet and vest
I'm brave as can be.
I'll ride this great bull
So much bigger than me.

The bucking begins
When the gate opens wide.
Raise my hand in the air
And we go for a ride.

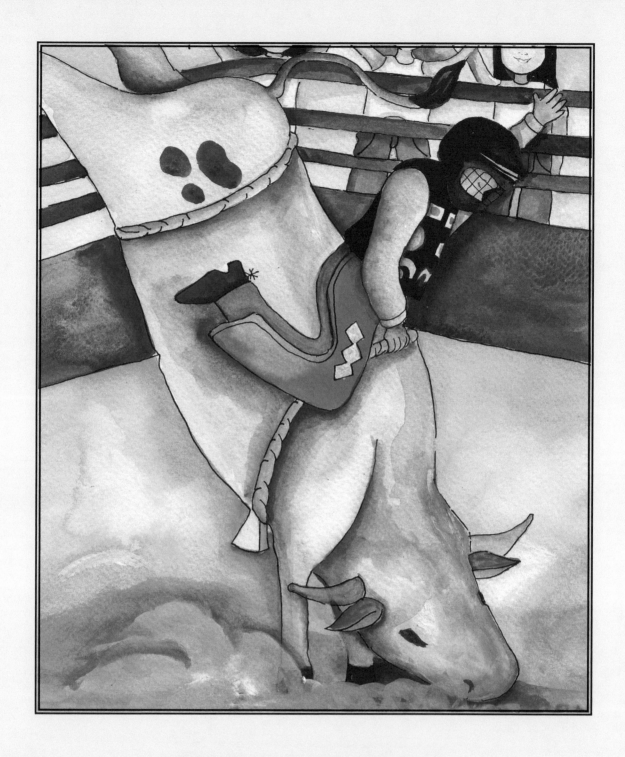

Just eight seconds to go
The bull twists with a buck.
I hang on real tight
'Cause I'm Buckaroo Chuck!

I know the ride's over
When the bell hits the ground.
Dirt and dust go a-flyin'
Then the clown comes around.

On that big bucking bull,
I rode with one hand.
I gave it my all.
I'M A RODEO MAN!!!

About the Author

Most comfortable in jeans and cowboy boots, Lexi Kinney is an LA city girl with a cowgirl's heart. Lexi has ten siblings, and is mother to five and granny to five. As the author of four picture books—*Buckaroo Chuck, Little Rosie Rodeo, Animal Jax* and *Little Joe Smileyhead*—she draws from her many life experiences to inspire children everywhere.

About the Illustrator

Born in Venezuela, Marianella Aguirre has been a world traveler since she was a young girl. She loved making sketches during travels with her mother and to this day many countries' cultures are reflected in her drawings. She has illustrated over twenty published books in both English and Spanish. Marianella and her husband currently reside in New Zealand.

CPSIA information can be obtained
at www.ICGtesting.com
Printed in the USA
BVHW020234030220
571171BV00003B/16

* 9 7 8 1 9 4 8 5 4 3 5 1 4 *